The Lost Sheep

by
Sharon Fear

illustrated by
René Mansfield

HOUGHTON MIFFLIN

Boston · Atlanta · Dallas · Geneva, Illinois · Palo Alto · Princeton

Little Bo Peep has lost her sheep
and doesn't know where to find them.

Where did those sheep go?

"Yoo hoo! Sheep!" cries Little Bo Peep.

"Where are you?"

Look! There they go!
They're getting on a bus!

4

And there goes Little Bo Peep.
She is right behind them.
"Stop, sheep!" she cries.
"Come back here!"

Look! There they go!
They're riding on a train,
and Little Bo Peep is behind them.

Here they come!
They're in a taxicab,
and Little Bo Peep is still behind them.

The sheep ride the elevator up.
Up goes Little Bo Peep, right behind them.
She's getting closer!

The sheep ride the escalator down.
Down comes Little Bo Peep, right behind them.
She's almost got them now!

Uh oh!
What are those sheep up to?
The first sheep jumps on a subway train.

The second sheep flies off in a helicopter.
But where is the third sheep?

There he is!
The third sheep is on a boat—
And Little Bo Peep is far, far behind him.

"Oh, no!" cries Little Bo Peep.
"Now I'll never find them."

Little Bo Peep has lost her sheep and
doesn't know where to find them.
But we know how to find them, don't we?

Just leave them alone
and they'll come home . . .

. . . wagging their tails behind them.